Matt Dickinson writes f teenagers. His books fo thrillers *Black Ice* and *H* bestselling account of his ascent of Mount Everest's deadly North Face, *The Death Zone*. For young adults, he has written an action-packed series called Mortal Chaos, and the stand-alone thriller *Lie, Kill, Walk Away*.

As a film-maker, Matt has worked extensively for National Geographic Television, the Discovery Channel and the BBC. He is one of very few people to have ever filmed on the summit of Mount Everest.

About Diffusion books

Diffusion publishes books for adults who are emerging readers. There are two series:

 Books in the Diamond series are ideally suited to those who are relatively new to reading or who have not practised their reading skills for some time (approximately Entry Level 2 to 3 in adult literacy levels).

 Books in the Star series are for those who are ready for the next step. These books will help to build confidence and inspire readers to tackle longer books (approximately Entry Level 3 to Level 1 in adult literacy levels).

Other books available in the Diamond series are:

Uprising by Alex Wheatle

Space Ark by Rob Childs

Fans by Niall Griffiths

Breaking the Chain by Darren Richards

Lost at Sea by Joel Smith

Books available in the Star series are:

Not Such a Bargain by Toby Forward

Barcelona Away by Tom Palmer

Forty-six Quid and a Bag of Dirty Washing by Andy Croft

Bare Freedom by Andy Croft

One Shot by Lena Semaan

Nowhere to Run by Michael Crowley

Snake

Matt Dickinson

First published in Great Britain in 2017

Diffusion
an imprint of SPCK
36 Causton Street
London SW1P 4ST
www.spck.org.uk

ISBN 978-1-908713-12-4
eBook ISBN 978-1-908713-23-0

Typeset by Manila Typesetting Company
First printed in Great Britain by Ashford Colour Press
Subsequently digitally reprinted in Great Britain

eBook by Manila Typesetting Company

Produced on paper from sustainable forests

Contents

1   Rattler   1

2   Rory's plan   7

3   Dead and gone   12

4   Katie   18

5   Chewy and Shiny Head   24

6   More questions   30

7   The medals   35

8   Bad news   41

9   Roasted snake   46

10   Freedom   52

1
Rattler

There aren't many shops left on the High Street any more. Most of them have closed down. All there is now are charity shops and bookies.

But there is still one shop left. It's a pet shop.

The shop is run by old Mr Nash. No one knows how old he is but they say he lived through the war. His beard is snow white and he wears wellington boots even when it's not raining.

I sometimes hang around outside the shop. I started doing it a couple of years ago when I was still at school.

It's mostly kids that go in there. They buy rabbits and mice and stuff.

I don't want any of my mates to see me hanging around the shop but I can't keep away. I like checking out the snakes in the window.

I have always had a thing about snakes. I think they are much cooler than any other pet.

The snake I really like has red, black and yellow bands. It looks really dangerous, just like a snake should. It eats baby mice. Yuck! But that's nature, I suppose.

One day I was looking in the window and Mr Nash opened the door.

'Hey,' he said. 'You are always hanging around out here.'

I thought he was going to tell me to get lost, but then he said, 'Why don't you come in and take a closer look?'

I went in and we got talking about the snake. After a while he asked, 'What's your name?'

'Liam,' I told him.

'Are you brave enough to hold a snake?' he asked.

You bet I was!

Some people think that snakes are slippery and slimy, but they are not. The snake felt dry and cool. It was beautiful.

'Scarlet kingsnakes and coral snakes can easily be confused,' Mr Nash told me, 'because they both have black, red and yellow bands.'

The snake started to curl round my arm. It was about four feet long and very strong. I could feel the power of it.

'One of them is poisonous,' the old man said, a twinkle in his eye. 'And the other isn't. I can teach you a rhyme so that you will remember which is which.'

'Go on then,' I said.

'Red on black, friend of Jack. Red on yellow, kills a fellow,' said Mr Nash.

I looked down at the snake on my arm. Its red bands were next to its black bands. That was OK then.

The snake was squeezing tighter. I had to laugh out loud. It was the strangest feeling. It was tickly, but also kind of scary.

'What you've got is a kingsnake,' Mr Nash said.

'Kingsnakes are not poisonous but they are tough. They can even kill rattlesnakes.'

I thought that was really cool. I loved holding the snake. I felt a connection to it.

I started going to the pet shop three or four times a week on my way back from the job centre. I enjoyed it. Mr Nash always gave me a cup of tea. He liked a good chat. One time he even showed me his war medals. He kept them in a special case on his desk.

Mr Nash would let me hold the kingsnake and sometimes I would clean out its cage. I even gave him a name, Rattler.

So why didn't I buy him? The problem was that Rattler cost more than a hundred quid, plus the cost of his cage, food and other stuff. I didn't have that kind of money. I have been signed on for months and I'm paying my mum rent.

I would love to see my mum's face if I came home with a snake. She would go bananas!

I reckoned I would have to wait until I got a job and a place of my own. Meanwhile I was hoping Rattler wouldn't get sold.

Then one day, I went to the shop as usual and it was closed. The shutters were down.

What do you think?

- What does Liam like about the snake?

- Why doesn't Liam want his mates to see him hanging around outside the shop?

- Why do you think Mr Nash invites Liam inside?

- Have you ever had to save up to buy something you really wanted? How did you feel when you finally got it?

2
Rory's plan

At first I didn't worry too much. I thought Mr Nash might be taking a break. But I was surprised because he never told me he was going away.

Two days went past. I was busy doing other stuff. I was trying to get an apprenticeship at an electrical company and I had a week of training.

It was great to get my hands on some proper work. I had been signing on for nearly two years and it was doing my head in.

But I still walked past the shop. And I kept remembering what it was like to hold Rattler. Two more days went by and I began to worry if anyone was going in there to care for the pets.

How long could Rattler go without water? How long could he live without food? What about all the other animals?

I banged on the shutters a few times but no one came. I began to think that Mr Nash must be sick. He had often been a bit breathless and once or twice I had seen him holding his chest.

I wished I had got a mobile number for him. I tried calling the shop but the phone just rang and rang.

I talked to my mum but she didn't seem bothered.

On the fourth day I was down there and this friend turned up. I say friend, but really I mean someone I know.

His name is Rory and he was in my class when we were at school.

Rory is a bit of a nutter. He's heavily inked and has a shaved head. He spends half his time in the kung fu gym and the other half down the nick. He was chucked out of school for fighting.

I hadn't seen Rory for months. I had heard that he had been sent away to a young offender institution for nicking a car.

'Mate!' he said. 'What's going on?'

He punched my arm. It was a bit too hard.

I told him about the pet shop being closed and said I was thinking about calling the police.

'The cops?' he said. 'Are you having a laugh? That's the last thing you should do.'

'What about the animals? They might be dying,' I said.

Rory lit a cigarette and took a big draw. 'We can go in the back,' he said. 'It's no big deal. We can just check it out.'

He made it sound so easy and so normal.

And like the mug I am, I said, 'OK, let's try it.'

Rory nipped home to get some tools. We went to the car park behind the shop and waited until there was no one around. My heart was thumping like mad.

Five minutes later we were over the wall. Rory broke the lock on the back door in a flash. All it took was one smash with a hammer.

The door swung open. I waited for an alarm to go off. But it didn't.

We stepped in. We heard a noise from inside but it was just the animals moving.

I bit on my lip. My body was shaking but I didn't want Rory to see it.

I turned on the torch on my phone. We walked slowly down the corridor and went into the shop.

What do you think?

- How do you think Liam feels about signing on?

- Why does Liam agree to Rory's plan to break into the shop? What else could he have done?

- Have you ever agreed to do something that you knew wasn't a good idea? Why did you agree?

- Why is it so hard to say 'no' to some people?

3
Dead and gone

Old Mr Nash was lying flat out on the floor. His face was grey. His body was stiff. His eyes were half open. It was really spooky.

We stood there for a few seconds. I didn't know what to say.

'Awesome!' Rory said in a whisper. 'The old geezer snuffed it.'

I had never seen a dead body before. I felt myself choking up but I couldn't let Rory see me cry.

'He was good to me,' I said. 'It's not right, him lying there like that.'

'He doesn't care about anything any more,' Rory said. 'No point in going on about it.'

I went to check out Rattler. As I got nearer he started moving. His tongue was darting in and out. I thought he was OK. I got him some crickets to eat and filled up his water bowl.

The rest of the animals were still alive so I went to sort them out too.

'You had better watch out for your prints,' Rory said.

'What?' I asked.

'Your fingerprints,' he said. 'If the police see your prints everywhere, they will think you killed the old geezer.'

'What?' I said. His words gave me a sick feeling in my throat.

This was getting well dodgy. Could we really be in the frame for murder? Surely Rory was just trying to scare me. Wasn't he?

'Let's check the till,' Rory said.

'The till?' I said. My brain was numb.

'There has got to be some cash,' said Rory.

Rory was beginning to sound angry with me. He went over to the counter.

'Nice.' He counted out a pile of notes with a big smile on his face. 'Sixty quid. Not bad.'

'What are you doing?' I said. My mind really wasn't keeping up with Rory.

'That's thirty for me,' Rory said. 'Thirty for you.'

Then Rory spotted the medals.

'Result!' he said. 'We can have them as well. They will be worth a bit.'

'Erm,' I began. 'I'm not sure we should be doing this.'

Rory spun round. He stared at me. 'Not going chicken on me, are you?' he asked.

'Course not,' I said. 'It's just that we have got to call the police and they will see the money and the medals are missing.'

'Why do we have to call the police?' Rory asked crossly. 'We take the gear and get out of here. End of story. Let the old guy rot.'

I felt my cheeks getting hot.

'We can't do that,' I told him. 'What about his family?'

'Oh yeah, like they really care!' Rory replied.

'Do you see the old guy's family trying to find out what's going on? They don't care about him and neither do we.'

I told Rory I didn't want the cash or the medals but I decided to take Rattler.

I found a bag with a zip and put Rattler in it. We left the shop, shutting the back door as best we could, and then went back over the wall.

I said goodbye to Rory and headed home.

As soon as I got home I got online and found a second-hand tank for Rattler from a guy across town.

I told Mum I was given the snake by a friend. She didn't freak out about it. In fact, she hardly seemed to care.

That night I couldn't sleep.

Every time I closed my eyes I saw a picture of old Mr Nash lying dead on the floor. How many more days would he be there? Surely his family would realize before long that he was missing?

It all felt wrong.

What do you think?

- How does Liam feel when he sees Mr Nash's body? How does Rory feel?

- Why do you think Liam refuses to take the money and the medals but takes the snake?

- Once they have broken in and found that Mr Nash is dead, what choices does Liam have about what to do next?

- Have you ever felt that you had 'no choice'? Looking back, was this really the case?

4
Katie

The next morning, I set out for work.

My week of training was almost over. The next day the boss was going to decide if I would get an apprenticeship. It was between me and another lad. My skills were better than his so I thought I would get it.

It was great to think I would soon be earning some money.

As I walked past the pet shop my heart did a back-flip.

There was a crowd of people outside the shop, and there was an ambulance and a police car. The shutters were open. There were police officers going in and out.

A girl my age caught my eye. She was in a pretty green dress but her face was as white as chalk.

'What's going on?' I asked her.

She took out a tissue and wiped away tears.

'It's my grandad,' she said. 'He has died.'

'Old Mr Nash?' I asked, trying to sound surprised.

'Yeah,' she said. 'I told my dad something was wrong but he wouldn't listen. We should have come down days ago.'

'Oh no,' I said. 'I'm sorry.'

I stood there like an idiot. I didn't know what else to say.

'Did you know him?' she asked.

Two ambulance men carried out the body. It was inside a special white bag. The crowd went quiet. I felt a big lump in my throat.

'I used to go in the shop when I was a kid,' I told her. 'Everyone round here knew him. He was always kind to us.'

'Yeah, he was a good person,' she said, wiping her eyes again.

A man walked over. I guessed it was her dad. He gave the girl a big hug.

'It looks like his heart just failed,' he said. 'But there's one thing that doesn't add up.'

'What?' she asked.

I got a sinking feeling in my guts.

'The shop has been broken into,' he said quietly.
'Someone got in through the back door and they
have taken what was in the till.'

'Was it a break-in gone wrong?' the girl asked.
'Do they think someone attacked him?'

'Who knows,' her dad said sadly. 'But the
police will get to the bottom of it. They are
fingerprinting in there now.'

Fingerprints! How careful had Rory and I been?

Suddenly I felt really stupid. Breaking in with
Rory was a really bad idea. I should have called
the cops when I realized something was wrong.

What if there were security cameras in the shop?
We hadn't even thought about that! We were
idiots! Total idiots!

I saw Rory standing on the edge of the crowd.

I flashed him a look to warn him away. The last thing I needed was him around.

'Hey,' I said to the girl. 'What's your name?'

'Katie,' she said. 'What's yours?'

'Liam,' I told her.

I checked my watch and said I had to go. I would have to run to get to work on time. It was a good couple of miles across town.

I got there just in time.

'Are you all right?' asked the boss. 'You are sweating like a pig.' He gave me a bit of a look.

'I'm fine,' I told him. 'I missed my bus, that's all.'

I could feel him watching me as I walked away to start work.

What do you think?

- How does Liam feel about breaking into the shop now that he knows the police have been called in?

- How has meeting Katie and her dad made a difference to the way Liam feels?

- What do you think Liam should do next?

- What would your dream apprenticeship be? What could you do to help achieve that dream?

5

Chewy and Shiny Head

I messed up a few times at work that day. I made some stupid mistakes. I just couldn't stop thinking about old Mr Nash.

When I got home that night, I took Rattler out of his tank. There was something calming about the feel of him moving up my arm. Rattler wasn't bothered by anything. Holding him made me feel the same.

I had just sat down to eat when the doorbell rang. Mum went to the door, and then she came back in a real flap.

'It's the police,' she told me. 'They want a word with you.'

I pushed my food away. Suddenly I wasn't hungry.

Mum looked at me crossly. 'What have you done?' she said.

'Nothing,' I said.

The two coppers were sitting on the sofa. They were big men and they did not look friendly. One of them had drops of sweat on his shiny head. The other was chewing gum non-stop.

'It's about Mr Nash,' Chewy said. 'We have just got a few questions for you.'

'We have had a look at the security camera on the High Street,' Shiny Head said. 'And we can see that you go into the shop almost every day.'

I kept my mouth shut.

'You might have been the last person to see Mr Nash alive,' said Chewy. 'Was there anything strange about him? Was he sick? Did he say he felt ill?'

'No,' I said. 'He looked all right.'

'Was there anyone hanging around the shop?' Chewy asked. 'Did you see anything unusual?'

'No,' I said.

'There's just one more thing,' said Shiny Head. 'We need to take your fingerprints.'

'Yeah?' I asked. 'What for?'

'There was a break-in at the shop,' Shiny Head said. 'It's just to rule you out.'

They took my prints. Mum was watching, biting her nails. I was trying to play it cool but my hand was shaking.

'Have you got any pets?' asked Chewy in a friendly way.

'He's got a snake,' Mum said. 'It's an evil-looking thing.'

I looked at Mum, trying to warn her to shut up. I really didn't want her to say anything more about the snake.

'I can't stand snakes,' said Shiny Head.

'He's only had it two days and I can't wait to get rid of it,' Mum said.

'Two days?' Chewy said. He frowned and flashed a look to his buddy.

'Yeah, I got it from a mate,' I told them. 'He joined the army and went away so he gave it to me.'

The two cops stared at me. I could not tell what they were thinking. I felt my face go red.

'That's all for now,' Chewy said. 'Call us if you think of anything else that might help.'

He left a card. The two men drove away into the night.

I called Rory to tell him the cops had been round.

'Mate,' he said. His voice was icy. 'You didn't tell them about me, did you?'

'Of course not,' I told him.

'Just checking,' he said. 'Because that would piss me off big time.'

'I won't tell them anything,' I said.

'Just keep your head down and it will all blow over,' he told me.

The next day was my big test at work. But I didn't sleep a wink that night.

What do you think?

- What do the police think of Liam? Do you think they believe that Liam got Rattler from a friend? Why or why not?

- How would you describe the relationship between Liam and his mum? (You may want to look over this chapter and the earlier chapters in the book.)

- Why can't Liam sleep that night?

- What are some good things to do if you are feeling stressed or can't sleep?

6

More questions

The next morning, when I was on my way to work, I saw Katie outside the pet shop again.

She was with her dad. They were cleaning out the shop and taking away the pets. Katie still looked sad but I could see she was feeling a bit better.

'How's it going?' I asked her. 'Do you need a hand?'

'Thanks,' she said. 'That would be great.'

I helped them to load their van with all the animals I knew so well.

While we worked Katie told me stories about her grandad. She said he had been a real hero in the war. I had never known that about Mr Nash.

Normally I feel shy around girls but with Katie it was different.

'The hardest thing is that Grandad's medals were stolen,' she said. 'He was so proud of them. My dad would do anything to get them back.'

We finished putting the cages in the van.

'What's your mobile number?' I asked her.

She gave me the number. I reckoned I would ask her out, after all this stuff died down.

Half an hour later I was at work. 'This is your big moment,' the boss told me. 'You will do a test at midday.'

Soon the waiting would be over. I would know if I had the apprenticeship or not.

Then, at eleven thirty, I saw a police car pull up outside. The same two cops as yesterday climbed out. And I knew that was really bad news.

The police took me into the company office. All the workers saw what was going on. The boss had a face like thunder.

'Your fingerprints match prints from the back door of Mr Nash's place,' Chewy said. 'You broke in there, didn't you?'

'I was in there nearly every day,' I said. 'I was always helping Mr Nash. My prints must be everywhere.'

'Do you know Rory Clark?' asked Shiny Head.

'Yeah,' I said. 'I was at school with him.'

It worried me that the police were asking about Rory. How did they know he was involved?

A hundred other questions followed. I never admitted a thing. I never dropped Rory in it.

'We are still looking for Rory,' Chewy said. 'He left his mum's house a few days ago and no one knows where he has gone. Can you help us with that?'

'No,' I told them.

'What about that snake of yours?' asked Shiny Head. 'You say your mate gave it to you. Can you tell us his name? How can we contact him to check out your story?'

I panicked. I made something up and gave them a false name.

The police left. My head was spinning. So were my guts. I felt so bad I had to go to the toilet.

When I came out, I asked the boss if I could still do the test. He gave me a hard look.

'We are going to let you go,' he said. 'We gave the job to the other lad.'

What do you think?

- Why does Liam offer to help Katie and her dad clear out the shop?

- Why are Mr Nash's medals so important to his family?

- Why do you think Liam is covering for Rory? What else could he do?

- Why do you think the other lad gets the apprenticeship and not Liam? Do you think this is fair?

7
The medals

I left work and went home early. Mum was surprised.

'Didn't you have your big exam today?' she asked.

'I'm feeling sick,' I told her. 'They said I could do it next week.' I didn't have the heart to tell her the truth.

I went to my room and lay on the bed. How much worse could things get?

I had lost the apprenticeship. The police were on my case. And, if the police found Rory, he would land me in it to try to save his own skin. It was a total mess.

I took Rattler out of his tank. But even he was in a bad mood. He didn't want to be handled. He hissed at me like I was an enemy.

I thought about Katie. I pulled out my mobile. I was about to call her but then I lost my nerve.

I thought about the medals that Rory had taken. What if I could get them back to Mr Nash's family? That would be something good I could do.

I went out and started asking around about Rory.

It wasn't long before this girl I know told me what the police hadn't been able to find out.

Rory was shacking up with a girl from our old school called Sally.

I took a bus over to Sally's place. It was in a rough part of town. I banged on her door and after a while Sally opened it.

I was shocked to see that she had a baby in her arms. She had kept that quiet. Her skin was grey. Her hair was greasy. I felt a bit sorry for her.

'I'm looking for Rory,' I told her.

'He will be back soon,' she said. 'You can come in and wait if you like.'

We went into the lounge. Sally lit up a cigarette and the baby started crying.

'Do you fancy a beer?' she asked.

'No, thanks,' I said. 'A cup of tea would be good.'

Sally went to the kitchen.

I knew I had to act fast. There was only one bedroom in the flat. I was in there in a flash. At first all I could see was dirty clothes and a mess of a bed.

'Do you want sugar?' Sally called from the kitchen.

I kept quiet. My heart was skipping like mad.

'Liam?' she called again.

Then I saw a kit bag. I unzipped it. The medals were right there. I grabbed them and made a dash for the front door.

Sally came into the room.

'Hey! Where are you going?' she cried. 'What's that in your hand?'

'Sorry!' I called back. 'Tell Rory I will call him!' I slammed the door behind me.

Rory was going to kill me. I knew that. But it still felt right to get the medals back.

I rushed back across town. When I was on the bus, I called Katie.

'Hey,' I said. 'It's Liam. Remember me?'

She did remember. She even sounded happy to be getting the call.

'I have got something for you,' I told her. 'Well, it's for you and your dad. Can I meet you in the park later?'

What do you think?

- What do you think Rory will say to Sally when he gets back and finds that the medals have gone? What will he say and do to Liam?

- Why do you think Liam has taken the medals from Rory?

- Do you think Liam has made a good choice or bad choice? Why?

- Can you think of a time you tried to right a wrong? Did it work out well?

8
Bad news

I had asked Katie to meet me in the park at seven o'clock. I was already there when she arrived. She was wearing a white summer dress and she looked great.

'Hey,' she said. 'It's not every day a boy turns up on time.'

We sat on the swings. I didn't mess around. I took the medals out of the plastic bag and gave them to her straight away.

'Awesome!' She gave a big grin.

It was the first time I had seen her smile. It was worth the wait.

'That's amazing!' she said. She looked at them closely. Then she stopped smiling. 'But where did you get them?'

'Contacts,' I told her. 'It may be better not to ask.'

She grabbed my swing and stopped it. 'I *am* asking,' she said.

I started talking about something else. I told her stupid stuff about the games I used to play in the park when I was a kid.

My mobile was vibrating against my thigh every minute or so. I didn't need to look at it to know who was trying so hard to get hold of me.

'Don't change the subject,' Katie said. 'Tell me the truth.'

Her eyes were really blue. They were the type of eyes it is hard to lie to.

Something inside me broke. I told her the whole story. I told her every last bit, right down to stealing the snake. She went quiet, just looking out across the park.

'I shouldn't have nicked the snake,' I said. 'I wasn't thinking straight. It was only because that snake was special to me.'

'You think I care about a snake?' she said. 'When you left my grandad lying dead on the floor?'

I watched a tear run down her cheek.

'How do I know you didn't scare him to death?' she said. 'I have only got your word for it that he was dead when you broke in.'

'I promise you,' I said. 'The shutters were down for days before we went in.'

'Great! Like it makes me feel better to know that Grandad was lying dead on the floor all that time,' she said. 'And how long after you broke in were you going to leave him there before you told anyone? You are such an idiot.'

I chewed on my nails. Now I couldn't look her in the face. My mobile vibrated again.

'Then you give me back the medals that you stole in the first place,' she said, 'like that makes you some great hero. Like I'm going to forgive you for not telling anyone my grandad was dead? You think we are going to be friends, when you have pulled all this crap?'

She threw the medal case on to the grass.

We sat there not saying anything for what felt like for ever. In my pocket, I felt my mobile vibrating away like crazy but I didn't get it out.

'Who is this Rory, anyway?' she asked. 'And how come you are friends with him? He sounds like really bad news.'

I saw three people coming towards us across the park. I felt the sour taste of sick in my throat.

'You will find out in a moment,' I said. 'Here he is.'

What do you think?

- Do you think Liam is right to tell Katie the whole truth? Why or why not?

- Do you think Katie is right to be so angry with Liam, or should she just be happy that he got the medals back?

- How important is honesty in a relationship?

- Mr Nash's family are proud of his medals and what they mean. What are you most proud of?

9
Roasted snake

We stood up and watched Rory and his two mates come towards us.

'You had better get out of here,' I told Katie. 'This is going to get nasty.'

She turned and ran towards the shops. I saw that she had left the medals on the ground but by then the three thugs were with me.

'Mate,' Rory said. 'We just want a word.'

I stood my ground. My legs were shaking. Then I saw that Rory was carrying something in his hand. It looked like a pillow case.

'We have just been to your place,' Rory said.

I really didn't like the sick smile on Rory's face. And his two mates were right hard cases.

'I guess your mum was out at work,' Rory said. 'But that didn't stop us from busting the door down and finding what I wanted.'

He held up the pillow case. Something was moving inside it.

Rattler! He had Rattler! I jumped forward to grab the bag, but he was too fast. He jerked it back as his friends blocked me.

'How do you like a taste of your own medicine,' he said with a nasty grin on his face. 'You think it's funny to break into my flat and steal my stuff?'

Rory pointed at the medals on the ground.

'I didn't break in,' I said. 'And you never should have nicked those medals in the first place.'

'No?' said Rory.

Now he looked really angry. Dangerously angry.

'You need to be taught a lesson,' he said.

He took a small tin from his pocket. For a second, I didn't know what it was. Then I understood. It was lighter fluid.

He began to squirt it on the sack. I rushed at him but his mates grabbed me. I was struggling like crazy but they held me tight. Rory pulled out a cigarette lighter. I could see Rattler was thrashing like mad inside.

'No!' I broke free for a second, using all my force.

Rory's mates slammed me to the ground. I got some hard kicks to my stomach and head. I held my arms over my head.

The smell of fuel filled the air.

'I like a bit of roasted snake,' Rory said and he laughed.

He clicked his lighter, once, twice. But it didn't light.

'You are sick!' I yelled.

'Hey!' came a shout.

Katie was back. She waved her smart phone in the air.

'I just got you on video and sent it to my dad,' she said. 'You three are so busted.'

Rory and the others looked at one another. They were gobsmacked.

'You *what?*' Rory said.

Katie walked right up to him. I couldn't believe her nerve. She grabbed Rattler out of Rory's hand and then bent down and picked up the medals.

Rory just stood there, his face white, his mouth hanging open.

'My grandad fought for these,' Katie said, pushing the medals in Rory's face. 'And now I'm fighting for them again. That's what he would want me to do and I'm not going to let him down.'

'I will remember this,' Rory said. 'And I will remember *you.*'

'Yeah?' she said. 'Big deal.'

He put his face really close to Katie's but she just stared him out.

'Come on,' Rory said to his mates. 'Let's leave these losers to their little pets.'

Rory and his mates walked away.

What do you think?

- Were you surprised by Katie's actions? How do you think she felt?

- Who do you think has been bravest in the story, Liam or Katie? Why?

- Have you ever had to stick up for something you believe in? How did you feel? Were you glad you did?

- What do you think is worth fighting for? How could you fight for it without using physical threats or violence?

10
Freedom

Katie helped me up from the ground. My whole body hurt from the kicking that Rory's mates had given me. I was spluttering from the pain in my ribs.

'You were awesome,' I said when I could talk. 'What made you come back?'

'The medals,' she said. 'I wasn't bothered about you.'

Then she smiled at me. I was happy to see that.

'Nice call on the video,' I told her. 'They will go down for GBH if that gets into the courts.'

I needed to check out Rattler. I hoped he wasn't hurt from being shaken or from the lighter fluid. I pulled him gently from the pillow case.

'Ow!' I cried, and dropped him. He had bitten me on the thumb. Needle-sharp pain ran up my arm. Rattler headed for the long grass.

'Stop him!' I yelled.

Katie made a dive. She missed him by an inch. I got his tail, but it slid out of my hand. Rattler slipped through a fence and into some wasteland.

There was no way I could follow him. The wasteland was covered in thorns and bushes that were way too thick for anyone to move in.

'That's it,' I said. 'He's gone.'

I was gutted. Katie looked at my thumb, which had two tiny bloody holes in it.

'You're not going to die, are you?' she asked.

'Red on black,' I told her. 'Friend of Jack. I'll be fine.'

I couldn't blame Rattler for making a break for it. After the way he had been treated, it was fair play. Getting dumped in a sack by that idiot Rory and squirted in lighter fluid was enough to make him hate humans for ever.

He saw his chance for freedom and he went for it.

*

My thumb was swollen for a few days. I had to have a tetanus injection in case the bite got infected. But it healed up pretty quickly.

Rory got sent down for six months. He had already done two spells in a young offender institution, so it was three strikes and he was out.

The judge was really angry about what Rory did to Rattler. She was more upset about Rattler than about the kicking that Rory's mates gave me. Cruelty to animals is a big deal in the courts.

I got forty hours of community service for breaking into the pet shop. I had to pick up litter all over town.

Sometimes I went looking for Rattler down by the wasteland.

Would he survive? Could he live in the wild? There were rabbits, mice and insects in those bushes, and snakes are natural hunters, so maybe he was OK.

I never saw him again. And there was never anything in the local newspaper to say that someone had been scared half to death by a snake.

Rattler had just vanished into thin air.

I didn't see Katie for ages. Then she came round on my birthday. I don't know how she knew it was my birthday.

She was carrying a big present. It was wrapped up and looked really special.

'Happy birthday,' she said.

I pulled off the paper. It was a glass tank. A beautiful black, red and yellow snake was inside.

'Great,' I said. My mouth went dry. 'Thanks a lot.'

Its bands were black on yellow.

'Just what I always wanted.'

What do you think?

- How did Liam feel about losing Rattler?

- What do you think of Rory? Do you think he gets what he deserves?

- What do you think Liam has learnt from the events in the story?

- If you could have any pet, what would it be and what would you call it?

Books available in the Diamond series

Space Ark
by Rob Childs (ISBN: 978 1 908713 11 7)

Ben and his family are walking in the woods when they are thrown to the ground by a dazzling light. Ben wakes up to find they have been abducted by aliens. Will Ben be able to defeat the aliens and save his family before it is too late?

Snake
by Matt Dickinson (ISBN: 978 1 908713 12 4)

Liam loves visiting the local pet shop and is desperate to have his own snake. Then one day, Mr Nash, the owner of the shop, just disappears. What has happened to Mr Nash? And how far will Liam go to get what he wants?

Fans
by Niall Griffiths (ISBN: 978 1 908713 13 1)

Jerry is excited about taking his young son Stevie to watch the big match. But when trouble breaks out between the fans, Jerry and Stevie can't escape the shouting, fighting and flying glass. And then Stevie gets lost in the crowd. What will Jerry do next? And what will happen to Stevie?

Breaking the Chain

by Darren Richards (ISBN: 978 1 908713 08 7)

Ken had a happy life. But then he found out a secret that changed everything. Now he is in prison for murder. Then Ken meets the new lad on the wing, Josh. Why does Ken tell Josh his secret? And could it be the key to their freedom?

Lost at Sea

by Joel Smith (ISBN: 978 1 908713 09 4)

Alec loves his job in the Royal Navy. His new mission is to save refugees from unsafe boats. But when a daring rescue attempt goes wrong, Alec is the one who needs saving. Who will come to help him?

Uprising: A true story

by Alex Wheatle (ISBN 978 1 908713 10 0)

Alex had a tough start in life. He grew up in care until he was fourteen, when he was sent to live in a hostel in Brixton. After being sent to prison for taking part in the Brixton Uprising, Alex's future seemed hopeless. But then something happened to change his life...

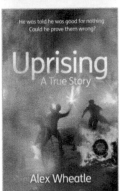

You can order these books by writing to Diffusion, SPCK, 36 Causton Street, London SW1P 4ST or visiting www.spck.org.uk/what-we-do/prison-fiction/